The Most Precious
of Cargoes

A Tale

JEAN-CLAUDE GRUMBERG

*Translated from the French
by Frank Wynne*

PICADOR

First published 2020 by HarperVia
an imprint of HarperCollins Publishers, New York

First published in the UK 2020 by Picador

This edition published 2021 by Picador
an imprint of Pan Macmillan
The Smithson, 6 Briset Street, London ECIM 5NR
EU representative: Macmillan Publishers Ireland Ltd, 1st Floor,
The Liffey Trust Centre, 117–126 Sheriff Street Upper, Dublin 1, DOI YC43
Associated companies throughout the world
www.panmacmillan.com

ISBN 978-1-5290-1958-2

Chapter motif woodcuts: Tugboat Printshop.

Typeset in Garamond Premier Pro by Palimpsest Book Production Ltd, Falkirk, Stirlingshire
Printed and bound by CPI Group (UK) Ltd, Croydon, CR0 4YY

MIX
Paper from
responsible sources
FSC® C116313

Visit **www.picador.com** to read more about all our books
and to buy them. You will also find features, author interviews and
news of any author events, and you can sign up for e-newsletters
so that you're always first to hear about our new releases.

The Most Precious of Cargoes

1

Once upon a time, in a great forest, there lived a poor woodcutter and the poor woodcutter's wife.

No, no, no, fear not, this isn't *Hop o' My Thumb*. Far from it. Like you, I hate that mawkish fairy tale. Who ever heard of parents abandoning their children simply because they could no longer feed them . . . ? It's absurd.

And in this great forest there reigned a great hunger and a great cold. Especially in winter. In summer, a sweltering heat beat down on the forest and drove out the great cold. The hunger, on the other hand, was constant, especially during those days when, all around the forest, the World War raged.

Yes, yes, yes, the World War.

The poor woodcutter had been conscripted to carry out public works – to the sole benefit of the conquering army that occupied the towns, the villages, the fields and the forests – and so it was that, from sunup to sundown, the poor woodcutter's wife trudged through the woodland in the oft-disappointed hope of providing for her humble family.

Fortunately – for it is an ill wind that blows no one any good – the poor woodcutter and his wife had no children to feed.

Every day, the woodcutter thanked heaven for this blessing. The woodcutter's wife, for her part, lamented it in secret.

True, she had no child to feed, but nor had she a child to love.

And so she prayed to heaven, to the gods, the wind, the rain, the trees, to the sun itself when its rays pierced the dense foliage and flooded her little glade with a magical glow. She implored the powers of heaven and earth to finally grant her the blessing of a child.

Little by little, as the years passed, she realized that all the powers, of heaven, of earth and of magic, were conspiring with her husband to deny her a child.

And so, she prayed that there might at least be an end to the hunger and the cold that tormented her from sunup to sundown, by night as by day.

The poor woodcutter rose before the dawn so he could devote all his time and energy to the construction of military buildings for the public – and the private – good.

Come wind, come rain, come snow, and even in the stifling heat I mentioned earlier, the poor woodcutter's wife roamed the forest, gathering every twig, every sliver of dead wood, stacking and hoarding it like some treasure once lost and now found again. She would also collect the few traps that her woodcutter husband set every morning on his way to work.

The poor woodcutter's wife, as you can imagine, had little leisure time. She wandered the forest paths, hunger gnawing at her belly, her mind reeling with yearnings she could no longer find words to express. She merely beseeched heaven that, if only for a single day, she might eat her fill.

The woods, *her* woods, her forest, stretched into the distance, lush and leafy, as indifferent to cold as to hunger, but, at the outbreak of this World War, forced labourers with powerful machines had slashed her forest from end to end and, in the gaping wound, had laid a railway line so that now, winter and summer, a train, a single train, came and went along this single track.

The poor woodcutter's wife liked to it watch pass, this train, *her* train. She watched expectantly, imagining that she too might travel, might tear herself away from this hunger, this cold, this loneliness.

Little by little, she came to organize her life, her daily routine, around the passing of this train. It was not a train of pleasing aspect. Crude timber wagons, each fitted with a single barred window. But since the poor woodcutter's wife had never seen a train, this one suited her fine, particularly given that, in answer to her questions, her husband had scathingly dismissed it as a cargo train.

'Cargo' – the very word warmed the heart and sparked the imagination of the poor woodcutter's wife.

Cargo! A cargo train ... She pictured wagons filled with food, with clothes, with fantastical objects, she imagined wandering through the train, helping herself, sating her hunger.

Little by little, excitement gave way to hope. One day, perhaps one day, tomorrow, the day after, it hardly mattered when, the train would take pity on her in her hunger and, as it passed, bless her with some of its precious cargo.

She soon grew bolder, and would go as close to the train as she dared, calling out, flailing her arms, pleading at the top of her voice or, if she was too far away to reach it in time, she would simply wave.

From time to time, a hand would appear at one of the windows and wave back. And from time to time one of those hands would throw something to her and she would rush to pick it up, giving thanks to the train and the hand.

Most of the time, it was nothing more than a crumpled scrap of paper which she would carefully, reverently, smooth out and then fold again and place next to her heart. Was it the sign of some gift to come?

Long after the train had passed, when night was gathering, when hunger was nagging, when cold was biting harder, she would feel a pang in her heart and would once more unfold the paper and, with pious reverence, gaze upon the illegible, indecipherable markings. She did not know how to read or write in any language. Her husband, for his part, knew a little, but she did not want to share with him or with anyone what the train had entrusted to her.

2

The moment he saw the cargo truck – a cattle wagon, to judge from the straw-covered floor – he realized their luck had run out. So far, as they were moved from Pithiviers to Drancy, they had been fortunate enough not to be separated. They had watched as others, those less fortunate, alas, departed, one after another, bound for who knew where, while they remained together. This period of grace, he believed, they owed to the existence of their beloved twins, Henri and Rose – Hershele and Rouhrele.

Truth be told, the twins had arrived at the worst possible moment, in the spring of '42. Was this the time to bring a Jewish child into the world? Worse, two Jewish children? Was it right to allow them to be born under a baleful yellow star? And yet, he believed, it was thanks to the twins that they had been able to spend Christmas 1942 together, in the internment camp at Drancy.

Better yet, thanks to their lucky star and to the Jewish administration of the camp, he had found work. He had almost completed his medical studies – specializing in eye, ear, nose and throat surgery – but in Drancy there were already many doctors, he was told, and many patients too – where there are Jews, there are many doctors and even more patients – but since two camp hairdressers had recently left ... Barber, perhaps? Very well, barber it would be.

It was pointless to split hairs, to try to understand, there was nothing left to understand.

So for as long as there were French gendarmes to guard them, he cut hair. He had so often watched his father wield his scissors, clicking at the air as though forewarning the hairs on the customer's head, as though launching an offensive, staring at the nape of a neck, utterly focused, then swooping down on an unruly lock, a tuft to be shorn with a decisive snip. Even professionally trained barbers took him for one of their own.

But after the gendarmes were replaced by the *verts-de-gris*, the Krauts, only members of the administration and a few internees required his services, a closely related and desperate clientele to whom he was forced to lie again and again. 'Of course, of course, it will be all right, everything will be fine, everything will be fine . . .'

In the spring of '42, yes, he had thought of aborting the child, not knowing at the time that they were two. But his wife, after much thought, decided she wanted to keep them. In time, she was delivered of two tiny Jewish babies, already registered, already classified, already marked out, already hunted, a little girl and boy, wailing in chorus, as though they already knew, as though they already understood. They have your father's eyes, his wife said. Yes, those first cries were heart-wrenching. Only their mother, overflowing with milk and with hope, could calm them. They soon ceased to wail in chorus and, later, trusting, continued to suckle in their dreams.

The tiny, discreet maternity clinic on rue de Chabrol, on the corner of Cité d'Hauteville, had even suggested they might keep the children and place them with a trustworthy family. 'What is a trustworthy family? What family could be more trustworthy than the one made up of their own father and mother?' Dinah had exclaimed, proudly hugging the twins to her breasts. She, who, despite the privations, despite Drancy, was producing milk enough for four, they said. She was brimming with milk, with love, with confidence. Would God have given life to these two cherubim if He had no intention of helping them to grow up?

And now, as the train juddered along, there she lay on the straw, cradling her two children, with no milk to feed them. Drancy had finally dried up her milk, her confidence and her hope. Here, amid the milling crowds, the panic, amid the screams and the sobs, the father, the husband, the phoney barber, the not-quite-doctor, the duly registered Jew, looked around for some place to shelter his family. As he looked around at his travelling companions, looked hard at them, he had a sudden realization. No, no, no, they were not being sent somewhere to work, those old men, that blind man, those children, his twins and the others. They were being sent far away, they were no longer wanted here, even marked, starred, registered, incarcerated, even stripped of their freedom, of everything, even then they were no longer wanted.

So, they were being sent away. But where? Where in the world were Jews still wanted? What country would be prepared to welcome them? What country would have opened its arms to them in February 1943?

But this was not the problem. Dinah had no milk now, or very little. Drancy had dried up her breasts. The rumours, the departure of her parents, and later his father. They had left and there had been no word from them since. She lay sprawled on the floor where, only recently, there had been cattle or horses destined for the slaughterhouse. She had spread out the woollen Pyrenean shawl she had been allowed to keep, the shawl in which she usually swaddled the twins. Everywhere was marked by cold, by war, by fear. When she lulled one twin, the other cried. When she rocked the other, the first one whimpered. They were two beautiful babies, a boy, a girl. 'The King's choice,' people said. 'The most beautiful babies in the world.' 'With those two, you have everything you could wish for.' 'I had three girls before I had my son! You already have one of each!' Where are they now? Everyone had offered up something from their memories, their sorrows, their rage. Their exhaustion, their fury. A woman sang a Yiddish lullaby. Dinah understood Yiddish, but pretended not to recognize it.

What could he do? What can I do? wondered the former ersatz barber. Until now, he believed, he had faultlessly fulfilled his role as father in the face of adversity. In spite of the difficulties, he had managed to protect his twins. He had pestered the camp administration. 'The twins! My twins!' They had become everyone's twins, the twins who had to be saved, protected, and now this . . . and now this. He felt powerless, helpless; he no longer knew what to do. He could not simply stand by and do nothing, he had to reassume his role, he had to find a solution. Two days they had been travelling already. The smell, the unbearable stench. The bucket in the corner of the wagon and the shame, the collective shame, the shame that had been deliberately engineered by those sending them who knew where.

First, they would be reduced to nothing, then to less than nothing, until there was nothing human left in them, so be it. But he had a duty to his children, he thought as he watched them suckle at their mother's dry breasts; he had to find a solution.

One of his fellow travellers asked whether he was Romanian. Yes, he was Romanian. The Romanian told him that he, too, used to be Romanian but now he was a stateless former Romanian. In this wagon there were many stateless former Romanians. They had been picked up in Paris or elsewhere in France. Someone mentioned Iași.

'You know Iași?'

'Of course I know Iaşi.'

'There was a pogrom there.'

'A pogrom? The war is raging there, just as it is here, there's no need for pogroms any more.'

'No, no, a pogrom. They loaded thousands of Jews onto a train at Iaşi, they set it rolling, and rolling, and rolling, until one by one the Jews aboard the train died of heatstroke, of thirst, of hunger.

'At every station where it stopped, the corpses were unloaded and the train moved on with the survivors. Sometimes, it went back the way it had come, moving in reverse. The train was not headed anywhere, this was the sole purpose of the journey: to stop at each station and unload . . .'

'The train we're on is moving, it isn't stopping. And besides, it's cold here, not hot.'

'It's just like Iaşi, I'm telling you. Just like Iaşi.'

Since then, every time the train stopped in a siding, he worried it would go back the way it came. That it would stop at a station and the dying, the children and the old men would be tossed onto the platform. He raged at himself. What could he do?

What could he do? Apologizing, he elbowed his way to the barred window. An old man was trying to catch his breath. Asthma, he said. The he smiled at the father of the twins. He nodded slowly and looked at him with eyes that seemed to know everything, with eyes that, since birth, had foreseen everything. He did not seem surprised; he just needed a breath of air.

Outside, the train had been slowed by drifts of snow. It suddenly stopped for a moment, then once more juddered into life, as though it, too, were suddenly asthmatic. It was then that it dawned on him.

Elbowing his way back through the crowd, he made his way to the woollen Pyrenean shawl. The important thing was not to choose, the important thing was not to think, but to scoop one of them up, without choosing between boy and girl. He took the child nearest to him. From his pocket, he had already taken his prayer shawl. The child was dozing. Dinah looked at him for a moment then she, too, closed her eyes and hugged the other twin to her.

As he made his way back to the window, he

unfurled the shawl. The bars – the bars were spaced widely enough for to squeeze an arm through. He could see the forest, the trees groaning beneath the weight of snow. He could see a figure who seemed to be running after the train, scurrying though the snow, and calling out.

He cradled the child, wrapped it in the tallit. The elderly asthmatic looked at him with eyes that seemed to say: Don't do it! Don't do it! Don't do what you are thinking of doing! But he was determined. Not enough milk for two. Perhaps enough for one?

Feverishly, he lifted up the infant swaddled in the shawl. Would the head fit between the bars? In Yiddish, the asthmatic said: 'Don't do it!' But the father looked at him and pretended he did not know a word of Yiddish. The head passed through; the shoulders followed. Then he waved at the old woman, who stopped and fell to her knees in the snow as though giving thanks to heaven.

The train roared out of the forest.

3

This morning, as every morning, early, very early, in the wintry half-light the poor woodcutter's wife is trudging, breathless, though the snow so as not to miss her train as it passes. She hurries, hurries, here and there stopping to collect branches that the weight of the snow and of the night have snapped and tossed onto the ground. She runs, she runs, pulling up feet shod with fox-cub pelts turned inside out and fashioned into boots by her poor woodcutter husband.

She runs, pulling the fox cubs from the snow. She runs, she runs, and when, finally, she arrives, breathless, at the clearing next to the railway track, she hears her train puffing, just as she is, panting, groaning, slowing, just as she is, hindered by the thick layer of snow that is slowing them both.

She waves her arms, shouting: 'Wait for me! Wait for me!'

The train pants and inches forward.

But this time, as it passes, it answers her. The cargo train – Convoy 49 – answers.

And not with a sign, but with a gesture. And not one of those gestures that accompany the miserable scraps of crumpled paper hastily scrawled on by some clumsy hand, no, a gesture, a real gesture. First, a flag appeared at the narrow window, brandished by a hand, whether human or divine, that suddenly lets it fall, and the flag drops its cargo onto the snow, some twenty paces from our poor woodcutter's wife, who falls to her knees, hands clasped to her breast, not knowing how to thank heaven. At last, at last, after all her unanswered prayers! But the hand at the window now reaches out towards her and with an imperious, peremptory finger, signals for her to pick up the package.

This package is for her. For her alone. It is meant for her.

The poor woodcutter's wife shrugs off her meagre bundle of winter firewood, she rushes over and lifts the small package from the snow. Then eagerly, feverishly, she unties the knots as one might unwrap a mysterious gift.

And there appears, oh miracle, the thing, the very thing for which she has longed and prayed for countless days, the thing she has dreamed of. But no sooner has the thing been unwrapped than the baby, rather than smile and reach out its arms as babies do in sacred images, the baby struggles, screams, balls its fists and, racked with hunger, thrashes and flails in its desperate desire to live. The package protests and goes on protesting.

Our poor woodcutter's wife hugs the little one to her, tucking it into her multi-layered scarves, and so she runs, and she runs, holding her treasure against her chest. Suddenly, she stops, she feels a hungry mouth attempt to suckle at her scrawny breast, then stop and start to howl again, wriggling, struggling, crying, wailing. The child is hungry, my child is hungry. She feels herself become a mother, at once blissfully happy and terribly anxious. Fulfilled, yet overwhelmed. Here she is, a mother, and a mother with no milk. My child is hungry, what can I do, what can I do? Why did the god of the cargo train not bless her with the milk to feed the child it has given her? Why? What were the gods thinking? How do they expect me to feed this child?

Back in her cabin, the small package laid on the bed writhes and squirms, driven by a strength born of despair, by the hunger of a wolf caught in a trap. The poor woodcutter's wife lights the fire, pours water into her kettle, and searches, searches, searches.

While the water is boiling, she finds some *kasha* that she can mix with the hot water, but first, to calm her little package, she presses a finger to the hungry mouth. The little package latches on, suckles, suckles with stubborn fury. Then, suddenly, realizing that it has been duped, it stops sucking and once more begins to howl. The poor woodcutter's wife, echoing its sobs, takes it in her arms as she mashes the *kasha* to make a buckwheat porridge that she tries to slip into the bawling mouth with a spoon. When this does not work, she dips her finger in the *kasha* and offers it to the baby, who now sucks eagerly, then releases the finger and spits out the bitter *kasha*.

The poor woodcutter's wife feeds it a little of the cooking water, then once again holds out her finger and the child sucks again. Little by little, as the cooking water quenches its thirst and the *kasha* staves off its hunger, the child in the arms of the new mother grows calm and the poor woodcutter's wife whispers a song in its ear, a lullaby that resurfaces from the shadowy past, surprising even her.

'Sleep, sleep my little cargo, sleep, sleep my own little bundle, sleep, sleep my own little child, sleep.'

Then she delicately sets her precious treasure in the hollow of the bed. Her eyes alight on the unfurled shawl, which she hangs on the end of the bed to dry. It is a magnificent shawl woven from slender threads, twined and knotted, fringed at both ends and embroidered with gold and silver threads.

Never has she seen or touched such a precious shawl. Truly, she thinks, the gods did well to wrap their gift in such rich material. Soon, she too dozes off with her little package, her precious little cargo clasped in her arms, wrapped in that magical shawl.

She sleeps, the poor woodcutter's wife, sleeps with her baby cradled in her arms, sleeps the sleep of the Just, she sleeps on high, high above the heaven granted to poor woodcutters and their wives, high above the Eden bestowed upon the fortunate, far above, far above, she in the garden reserved for gods and for mothers.

4

Night draws in, while the poor woodcutter's wife and her gift from heaven sleep, the poor woodcutter, worn out from his public works, returns to the cabin. At the noise he makes, the little cargo wakes, and finding its hunger unsated, immediately begins to cry.

'What on earth is that?' roars the woodcutter.

'A child,' says the poor woodcutter's wife, sitting up with her little package in her arms.

'What the devil do you mean, a child?'

'The joy of my life,' says the poor woodcutter's wife, without blinking or trembling.

'The what?'

'The gods of the train gave it to me.'

'The gods of the train?!'

'So that he might be the beloved child I never had.'

The woodcutter immediately grabs the little cargo, ripping him from the arms of the poor woodcutter's wife, which has the paradoxical effect of calming the wailing and the sobs of the baby, his frantic hands clutching at the husband's beard, which he tries to suck on.

'Don't you know what it is, this child? Don't you know?'

And suddenly, in disgust, he drops the child onto the bed as one might toss a piece of rotting meat into the bin.

'He stinks! Don't you know what race this brat belongs to?'

'I know that he is my own little angel,' the poor woodcutter's wife says, once more scooping the child into her arms. 'And he can be yours, too, if you choose.'

'That thing can never be an angel, yours, mine, or

anyone's. He is the offspring of the accursed race. His parents threw him from the train because they are heartless.'

'No, no, no. The gods of the train delivered him to me.'

'You're raving, woman, when he's grown, he will be as they are – heartless.'

'Not if it's us that raise him.'

'And how will you feed him?'

'He is so small, an hour ago I gave him my finger to suck and that was enough to calm his hunger.'

'Don't you know that to shelter the heartless is forbidden on pain of death? They are the ones who killed God.'

'Not him, not him! He's so small.'

'They killed God, and they are thieves.'

'Thank the Lord in this world we have never had anything to steal. And soon, if you are willing, he can help me fetch wood from the forest.'

'If they find him in our house, they will nail us to the wall.'

'Who will know?'

'The other woodcutters will betray us to the hunters of the heartless.'

'No, no, I will say that the baby is mine, that I finally grew big with child from your ministrations.'

'And you belatedly gave birth to a fifteen-pound monster?'

'We won't take him out at first.'

'We cannot make him ours, the child is marked.'

'What do you mean, marked?'

'Do you not know that the heartless are marked, that this is how they can be recognized?'

'Marked how?'

'Their nature is not like ours.'

'I saw no mark.'

The woodcutter busies himself unwrapping the little package so that it is revealed it in all its nakedness.

'See, see?'

'See what?'

'The mark.'

'What mark?' the poor woodcutter's wife asks, gazing at the child in turn. 'I see no mark.'

'Look at the lad – he is not made as I am.'

'No, but *she* is made as I am. See how beautiful she is.'

The woodcutter quickly turns away, then, having scratched his head beneath his cap, he sets about rewrapping the little package whose eager fists push away the assailing hands.

'What are you doing?' the poor woodcutter's wife says anxiously as she watches her husband pick up the package and stride towards the door. 'Where are you going?'

'I'm going to leave it next to the railway line.'

At this, the poor woodcutter's wife hurls herself at him in a fury and tries to snatch her little package from her husband. When this fails, she blocks his path and says:

'If you do that, husband, you will have to throw me with her under the wheels of the cargo train, and the gods, all the gods, of the heavens, of the earth, of the sun and of the train, will hunt you down wherever you go. Whatever you do. You will be cursed for good and for ever.'

The woodcutter's husband stands, motionless, for a moment. He returns the little cargo to his wife, the 'little lad' now a 'little lass' since her nature has now been revealed to us and that nature is unarguably female.

As the little cargo passes from hand to hand, amidst wails and fury, she too begins to shriek like a thousand muted trumpets.

The woodcutter, who is not, it seems, a music lover, instantly covers his ears and bellows:

'So be it! So be it! Let it be so and let all the misfortune that follows be your misfortune.'

The poor woodcutter's wife, hugging her little cargo to her, says:

'She will be my joy, and yours.'

'You can keep the joy to yourself, thank you. Much good may it do you. But know this: I don't want to hear her or see her ever again. Shut her up and consider yourself warned.'

As she rocks her little cargo, the poor woodcutter's wife goes out to the woodshed, where there are no floorboards, and settles there with the child the gods have given her to cherish. Hard on her heels, the woodcutter appears and tosses her a tattered bearskin that has been gnawed by field mice.

'Here! And don't you go catching a cold!'

'The gods will protect me,' the poor woodcutter's wife responds.

The child still sobs, now half asleep.

As he leaves the woodcutter growls:

'Shut her up! Or else . . .'

The poor woodcutter's wife carries on rocking the child, holding her tightly and peppering her forehead with the gentlest of kisses. And here they fall asleep, mother and child. A silence descends, one scarcely troubled by the mournful snores that issue from the nostrils of the poor woodcutter's wife, and the counter-point of contented sighs that rise from the little cargo, gift from God, and her new and loving mother, wrapped as they are in a tattered bearskin gnawed at by field mice.

5

The cargo train, designated by the bureaucracy of death as Convoy 49, having set off from the station at Bobigny, near Drancy, on 2 March 1943, arrived on the morning of 4 March in the pit of hell, its final destination.

Having offloaded its cargo of former tailors for gentlemen, ladies and children, both dead and alive, accompanied by their relatives, whether close or distant, along with their customers and their suppliers, not forgetting, for the devout, their ministers of religion, and for the invalids, the old, the sick and the impotent, their personal doctor, Convoy 49 – doubtless impatient to become

Convoy 50, or 51 – immediately set off the way it had come.

The poor woodcutter's wife did not see it roar past, empty, absorbed as she was in her new responsibilities as a mother.

Any more than she witnessed the passing of Convoy 50, or those that followed.

Once the cargo had been received, it was immediately subjected to a selection process. Having conducted their examination, the expert selectors – all qualified doctors – retained only ten per cent of the delivery. A hundred head out of one thousand. After treatment, in the late afternoon, the remainder – the rejects: the elderly, the men, the women, the children, the infirm – vanished into thin air or the boundless depths of the desolate Polish sky.

Thus it was that Dinah, registered as Diane on her provisional papers and her brand-new official family record book, and her child Henri, twin brother of Rose, slipped the surly bonds of earth and reached the heavenly limbo promised to the innocent.

6

In many fairy tales, and this is indeed a fairy tale, there is a forest. And in that forest, a grove denser than the surrounding woodland, one that can be entered only with difficulty, a wild, secret place protected from intruders by the vegetation itself. An isolated place where neither man, nor beast, nor god can enter without trembling. In the sprawling forest in which the poor woodcutter and his wife strive to subsist, there exists such a grove, a place where the trees are lusher, denser. A place spared by the woodcutter's axe, through which there is no path. A leafy copse into which one may steal only in silence. Children are not allowed to play there. And even their parents dare not set foot there for fear of being lost.

The poor woodcutter's wife, who knows these woods as she knows her pockets – the shawls in which she swathes herself in winter have no pockets, and if they did, she has nothing to put there – even so, let us say that she knows this place which, she believes, is the preserve of faeries and sprites, of witches and werewolves. She also knows that a lone human lives in here like a hermit, a creature that inspires fear and horror in everyone, one that even the Boches and their miserable conscripts dread encountering. Some say the creature is malevolent, others say he is a friend to animals and an enemy to man. The woodcutter's wife has glimpsed him only on days when she was gathering wood on the outskirts of this grove, over which he reigns supreme and solitary.

Alas, she also knows, has known since the early hours, that her little cargo cannot survive and prosper without milk.

After the woodcutter headed to work, she wrapped

herself in scarves into which she slipped her little cargo, enfolded in the shawl provided by the gods themselves, the shawl trimmed with gold and silver that might have been woven by a faerie hand.

Then she set off for that part of the forest where no one ventures without trembling and committing his soul to God's keeping. As she approaches the grove, she is met by the darkness that constantly reigns in this part of the forest. She waits and watches. Is the man here? Can he see her? What of the goat? Is the nanny goat still of this world? Does she still give milk?

Before setting out, she tried to feed her beloved little cargo a little *kasha* porridge. To no avail. The *kasha* was spat up. And now, the icy little head of the little cargo is nodding weakly. The child needs milk, she thinks, milk, milk, if not ... No, no! The gods cannot have granted her this child only for her to watch it die in her arms.

She ventures into the darkness, dipping under the low branches, calling on the gods of the train, the gods of nature, of forests, of goats. She entreats the faeries – one never knows – and even the mischievous sprites who, surely, would not stoop so low as to harm an innocent child. Come to my aid, come to my aid all of you, she whispers in the tangle of branches that crack beneath her feet. No one ever comes to gather wood here. The very snow dares not lie upon the ground. It melts in the treetops and settles on the boughs.

'Who goes there?'

The poor woodcutter's wife stops, petrified.

'A poor woodcutter's wife,' she says in a quavering voice.

The voice continues:

'Let the poor woodcutter's wife take another step.'

She freezes. The voice continues:

'What does she want, this poor woodcutter's wife?'

'Milk for her babe.'

'Milk for her babe?'

There comes a sound, a sinister laugh.

Then, with a creak of boots on rotten wood, a man appears, on his head a *czapka*, in his hand a rifle.

'Why do you not give her yours?'

'Alas, I have no milk. And if the child that you see,' she takes the babe from under her shawl, 'does not get milk this day, she will die.'

'Your daughter will die? What of it? You shall make another.'

'I am no longer of an age. And besides, this child was entrusted to me by the god of the cargo train that moves to and fro along the railway track.'

'Who gave you no milk to feed it with!'

Once more, he lets out a laugh bitter enough to chill the bones.

Fearful but determined, the poor woodcutter's wife says:

'He forgot. The gods cannot think of everything, they have so much to do here below.'

'And do they do it badly!' the man concludes.

Then, after a moment, he questions her again.

'Tell me, poor woodcutter's wife, where do you expect me to get milk?'

'From the teats of your nanny goat.'

'My nanny goat? How do you know I have such a thing?'

'I heard it bleating while I was gathering wood on the borders of your kingdom.'

He laughs again, then, gravely, composes himself and asks:

'What will you give me in exchange for my milk?'

'Everything I have.'

'And what do you have?'

'Nothing.'

'That's hardly an exchange.'

'All the days the gods give, I will come here, winter and summer, and bring a bundle of firewood in exchange for two mouthfuls of milk.'

'You want to pay me for my milk with my wood?'

'The wood is not yours.'

'Neither is it yours.'

'Just as your milk is not your milk.'

'What do you mean?'

'It is milk from your goat.'

'But the goat is mine. Nothing in life is given without recompense.'

'Without milk, my daughter will die, without recompense.'

'So many people die!'

'It was the gods who entrusted her to me, if you help me to feed her, she will live, they will be grateful, and they will protect you.'

'They have protected me more than enough already.'

He rips off his *czapka* to reveal a battered forehead, a crushed temple, and a missing ear.

'These days, I shun their protection and take care of myself.'

'But they have kept you alive, and your goat, too.'

'Small thanks.'

'I will bring you two bundles of firewood every day for a single mouthful of milk.'

'I can see you're well versed in business!'

He laughs again.

'Did the gods not give you some object of value when they gave you the little girl?'

Our desolate poor woodcutter's wife is about to

say, no, alas, when suddenly her face lights up. She frees her little cargo from the prayer shawl and proffers it to the man with the goat who eyes it scornfully.

'It is a divine shawl, see how intricate it is.'

The man wraps it around his neck.

'Look how beautiful it is! It must surely have been woven by faerie hands that embroidered it with silver and with gold.'

The little cargo whimpers softly. The loud wails are past, she no longer has the strength.

The man with the goat and the battered face surveys the child and concludes:

'This divine creature is hungry, like a common human child. I will give you a little milk from my goat. What you really need is milk from a jenny, but I have none now, so the milk I give you for the next three months must be diluted with boiled water, two measures of water to one of milk, and you should supplement her food with porridge and, come spring, with fruits and vegetables.'

He hands back the child. She takes her daughter

lovingly, then falls to her knees and tries to kiss the man's hand. The man recoils.

'Get up!'

Still on her knees, the poor woodcutter's wife lets her tears flow.

'You are a good man, a good man,' she murmurs.

'No, no, no, no. We have simply struck a deal. I will be expecting my firewood tomorrow morning.'

'Who broke your head, good man?'

'The war.'

'This one?'

'This or another. It hardly matters. Never kneel before me or before anyone else again, never let me hear you say I am a good man and never let others know that I have a goat or that I give you milk. Come, I will give you what you are owed.'

And so it came to pass.

Every morning, the poor woodcutter's wife brought a bundle of firewood and received in exchange a warm cupful of milk.

And this is how, thanks to the man in the woods and his goat, the poor little cargo, so miserable and so precious, endured and survived. And yet, she was never sated, hunger constantly gnawed at her. She would suck anything she could put in her mouth and, once restored to health, she howled without restraint.

7

Having no scissors, and armed only with a pair of shears, the father of the twins, the husband of Dinah, our hero, having vomited up his heart and choked down his tears, set about shaving and shaving the thousands of heads that arrived on cargo trains from the farthest reaches of the countries occupied by the murderous devourers of yellow stars.

These heads, these shears, the secret thought that perhaps, perhaps . . . for a short while, these things rendered him a survivor in spite of himself.

8

At nightfall, when the woodcutter would come home, dragging aching limbs and a body broken by a day spent labouring in the public interest, he did not want to see, still less hear, the small solitary twin. And so, the poor woodcutter's wife tried to get her to sleep before he returned. But sometimes it happened that the little one would moan or stir in her sleep. Sometimes, she would wake, sobbing from the nagging hunger, or howling in fear as though every wolf on earth had joined a monstrous pack that pursued her into the deepest depths of sleep.

At such times, the woodcutter would pound his

fist on the table, muttering into his beard in a voice made hateful by the moonshine he drank with his workmates: 'I don't want to see or hear that limb of Satan. That accursed offspring of the heartless! Shut her up, or I swear I will throw her to the swine.'

Fortunately, thought the poor woodcutter's wife, there were no longer any wild pigs in these woods, the hunters of the heartless having long since requisitioned and eaten them. Fortunately, too, the exhausted woodcutter would soon begin to nod off and slump down, with his head down on the table, there to sleep the sleep of the unjust.

9

And yet there came a night when, crying more than usual, the little cargo woke the woodcutter from his doze. In his great wrath, he went so far as to raise his hand to the child. The poor woodcutter's wife caught the calloused paw of her poor husband in mid-air, held it suspended for a moment, and then gently laid it on the chest racked with sobs of her beloved little cargo. Feeling his palm brush against this skin, so soft, so pale, the woodcutter tried to pull his hand from the grip of his wife, but she held it firmly in both hands against the little girl's ribcage, all the while whispering in the ear of her husband as he roared that he wanted nothing to do with this demon spawn, this cursed heartless creature, the poor woodcutter's wife, still gripping her husband's hand, gently whispered:

'Can you feel? Can you feel? Can you feel the tiny beating heart? Can you feel it? Can you feel it? It's beating. It's beating.'

'No! No!' cried the woodcutter's cap, fluttering wildly. 'No! No!' howled his bushy beard. 'No! No!'

Still whispering, the poor woodcutter's wife said: 'The heartless have a heart. The heartless have a heart like you and me.'

'No! No!'

'Man or child, the heartless have a heart that beats inside their chest.'

With a jerk of his shoulder, the woodcutter suddenly wrenched away his hand. He was still shaking his head, still hissing between clenched teeth, repeating the sad slogans of these dark days: the heartless have no heart! The heartless have no heart! They are stray dogs to be driven out with an axe! The heartless toss their children from the windows of passing trains and it is left to us, poor fools, to feed them!

As he spat his blackest bile, he felt a troubling confusion, a warmth, an unfamiliar gentleness that this fleeting contact of his palm with the warm skin and pulsing heart of the little cargo had kindled in his own heart which he now felt beating inside his chest. Yes, his heart was beating as though in time with the little heart of the little cargo, now finally calm in his wife's arms and reaching out her tiny hands towards the woodcutter.

The man recoiled in fear. When the woodcutter's wife held out the child to him, he recoiled again, as though struck full in the chest, all the while unthinkingly repeating that he did not want to have to look at the child, did not want to have to feed it, even as he struggled to consign to the depths of his being the urge to respond to those outstretched arms, to take the child and press her against his face, against his beard.

At length he regained his footing and, with it, his composure, and relaunched his attack, warning his poor wife that tomorrow she would have to choose between him, an honest man and her husband, and the misbegotten abortion of a Christ-killer she was holding in her arms. And before the poor woodcutter's wife could answer, he collapsed onto his bed and this time slept the sleep of the almost just.

10

The following day, no matter where he laid his hand, he felt the heart of the little cargo beating against his palm. In the silence of his heart that now brimmed with an unfamiliar tenderness, he too called the little heartless thing his own little cargo. And when on the rare occasion he found himself alone with her, he would hold out a hesitant finger which she would immediately clutch and refuse to let go of. In such moments, he felt a joyful and life-giving gentleness.

Indeed, one day, as the little girl was crawling on all fours on the floor of the hut, he grabbed the cuff of his trousers and, using both hands, she pulled herself to her feet, clutching one of the patched knees. The woodcutter could not stifle a cry: 'Oh, mother! Come! Come and see! Come and see!' The child, now holding on with only one hand, tottered, struggling to get her balance. The woodcutter was exultant: 'Look at her! Look at her!' The poor woodcutter's wife was also delighted and clapped her hands. The little girl tried to clap too, letting go of the patched trousers, and ended up on the ground, on her backside, in peals of laughter. The woodcutter, head over heels, scooped the child from the ground and brandished her like a trophy, squealing with joy and shouting Hallelujah!

In the days that followed, the woodcutter and the poor woodcutter's wife did not feel the yoke of time, nor the cold, the hunger, the penury or the wretchedness of their circumstances. The world seemed lighter and more secure despite the war, or perhaps because of it, thanks to this war that had given them the most precious of cargoes. All three shared a full bundle of happiness,

decorated with a few wildflowers that the bur-
geoning spring offered them to brighten their
home.

11

Bolstered by this joy, this happiness, the wood-cutter now worked with greater zeal, with greater strength. His comrades warmed to him more and despite his taciturn nature invited him more often to join their post-work libations. One of them, more enterprising then the rest, had set up a home still that produced wood alcohol. He provided the drink. I do not know the recipe of this home-made wood alcohol and, even if I did, I would not give it to you. Suffice it to say that drinking wood alcohol is not advisable and that it can, in large quantities, cause blindness. 'What matter, we'll just have to make the best of things, and besides it's not as though there's much worth seeing,' announced the amateur distiller. The comrades were brave and boozy. After the day's labours, they raised their glasses, since at home they did not have a little cargo bequeathed them by the train and by the heavens that might lead them to cherish life, if only their own.

After their labours – glug, glug, glug – on certain evenings, the woodcutter agreed to bend the elbow with his co-workers, reluctantly deferring the pleasure of returning to his beloved little cargo. In doing so, he shared his new-found happiness with his companions in misfortune – glug, glug, glug – and they would raise a glass, and then another. To what? To whom? One suggested they drink to the imminent end of this accursed war – glug, glug, glug – then they drank to the extermination of the heartless – glug, glug, glug – one comrade announced that the crowded train they had seen returning empty was transporting heartless creatures from the seven corners of the world. Another went further: 'Here we are, slogging our guts out for starvation wages, while the heartless are being ferried around for free on special trains!'

At length, a third man clarified: 'The heartless killed God, they brought about this war! They did not deserve to live and their accursed war will end only when the world is finally rid of them for ever!' – glug, glug, glug – 'To their demise!' – glug, glug, glug – 'To the death of the heartless!' – glug, glug, glug – they cheered in concert.

Not quite in concert . . .

Our poor woodcutter, husband to our poor wood-cutter's wife – since all were woodcutters and all were poor – our woodcutter drank but stayed silent. At once, the others turned to him, waiting to hear him speak. They did not have to wait long– glug, glug, glug – the woodcutter wiped his lips with the back of his hand then, in the silence, to his surprise, he heard himself speak.

'The heartless have a heart.'

'What, what, what? What did he say? What does he mean?'

And the woodcutter once again surprised himself.

This time in a thunderous voice that he had never before felt in his throat, the woodcutter, having slammed his tin cup down on the rickety table, causing it to collapse, said: 'The heartless have a heart.'

Then he set off at speed, though weaving a little, towards his hut, towards his home, his axe slung over his shoulder, suddenly terrified that he had bellowed his truth, the truth: the heartless have a heart. Terrified and at the same time relieved and proud, proud to have roared it into the faces of the others, to have freed himself, to have suddenly ended a whole life of submission and silence. He was heading home to his beloved wife, to the apple of an eye that the wood alcohol would not blind that evening. He was heading home to the precious cargo that the gods, for it could have been no one else, had bestowed on him. And, as he walked, he felt his heart pound and pound, then he was surprised to hear himself singing, singing as he walked, a song he had never sung, though nor had he ever sung another. He was walking and singing, intoxicated, drunk on freedom and on love.

His consternated comrades exclaimed: 'He can't hold his drink like he used to! He's drunk! He's off his head!' – glug, glug, glug – 'He'll be fine tomorrow when he's sober.' And they too began to sing, songs taught to them by their masters, by the hunters of the heartless, by the invaders, songs that said:

'We will plunge our knives into the hollow chests of the heartless until not one remains, until they have returned to us all the things they stole – death to the heartless' – glug, glug, glug—

And as he drank, the man who made the wood alcohol remembered how, before the war, the local authorities offered a reward for the head of every verminous animal that hunters brought to the town hall – glug, glug, glug.

12

The days passed; the months passed. The phoney barber, the father of the former twins, shaved, shaved and shaved. Then he gathered the hair, the blonde, the dark, the red, and fashioned it into bales. Bales that joined other bales, thousands of other bales. The highly prized blonde hair, the dark hair, even the red. What did they do with the grey hair? All this hair was shipped off to the land of the conquering generals to be fashioned into wigs, finery, upholstery or simple floor cloths.

The father of the former twins longed to die, but deep inside him a strange seed began to bud, a seed oblivious to the horrors he had seen, had suffered, a tiny seed that grew and grew, commanding him to live, or at least to survive. Survive. He ridiculed this tiny seed of hope, scorned it, drowned it in floods of bitterness, yet still it continued to grow, in spite of the present, in spite of the past, in spite of the memory of the senseless act that had meant that his beloved had not spoken another word to him until they alighted from the train of horror and were separated on that station platform with no station. He had not even been able to press his remaining twin to his chest even for a moment, before they were separated for ever and always. He would be weeping for them still, had his eyes been capable of tears.

13

The days passed, the months passed and, on a day happier than others, the little cargo suddenly stood up straight and took her first steps. Since then, she would trot ahead of or trail behind the poor woodcutter's wife all day, and at night, she would run to greet the woodcutter. And when he lifted her up to his face, to his beard, she would try to take off his cap, or tug at his hair or – joy of joys – grab his fat nose in both her hands. The woodcutter would feel his heartstrings jangle. Then he would hand the little cargo to the poor woodcutter's wife and loudly blow his nose before dabbing at his damp eyes. On one such day, more beautiful than the others, the little one ran to the woodcutter crying, 'Papa! Papa!' in the peculiar language spoken in that far-flung country where papa was *papouch*, mama was *mamouch*.

'*Papouch! Mamouch!*'

The three would throw their arms around each other, caught up in a single embrace that ended with laughter, or even with a song that told of father and mother, of a child lost and found.

14

One day, as the poor woodcutter's wife and her little cargo, having gathered their firewood, were trudging home through the undergrowth, they came face to face with the man who distilled the wood alcohol – incidental colleague and comrade of the woodcutter. Seeing the little one, the distiller politely enquired: 'Where did she come from, this little one?' The poor woodcutter's wife said that the child was hers. For a long moment, the distilled studied the little cargo, as though weighing her up. Then he stared at the poor woodcutter's wife before smiling and taking his leave, though not without raising his moleskin cap and cheerfully announcing: 'Good day to you both!'

15

One morning, shortly before dawn, the comrade in the moleskin cap, flanked by two militiamen weighed down with rifles from some earlier world war, or more plausibly from the time when the Chinese first invented gunpowder, all three, then, came to take delivery of the little cargo. The woodcutter greeted them at the threshold. At first, he denied the charges. He claimed it was his daughter. One of the militiamen asked why he had not registered the birth at the town hall. He answered that he did not like filling in documents and so the child had grown, undocumented. At length, on pain of death, he confessed – the law is the law, comrade – he confessed, as I say, but as a special favour, he asked that he might hand the child over to his comrade, so that what had to be done might be done gently, so that the rifles would not alarm the little one or, above all, his wife. He ushered his comrade inside, calling loudly to his wife:

'It's a comrade from the building site! Get the little one ready! And fetch our friends here a drink!'

The woodcutter's wife appeared, holding the child, who instantly reached out to the woodcutter, who snatched up his axe and swung it at the distiller, while screaming to his wife:

'Flee! Take the child and flee!'

Again and again he brought the axe down on the moleskin that adorned his workmate's skull. Then he stepped out of the cabin, his head held high, and lashed out at one of the militiamen. He felled the man like a rotten trunk. The other backed away, stumbled, fired a shot into the air, then aimed for the advancing woodcutter with his raised axe. His wife raced out even as the poor woodcutter crumpled, roaring:

'Run, my darling! Run! Save yourself! Save yourself! May God strike down all soulless, faithless men! And may . . .' his voice dropped to a whisper, '. . . may our little cargo live.'

16

Run run run poor woodcutter's wife! Run and clutch your fragile cargo to your heart! Run and do not turn back. No, no, do not look back at your poor husband as he lies in his own blood, or the three maggots split by his axe like rotten wood. No, no, do not glance back at the cabin that your woodcutter husband built with his bare hands from logs. Forget this cabin in which the three of you shared that all-too-fleeting happiness.

Run? But where? Where to run? Where to hide?

Run without thinking! Go, go, go! Run straight ahead, do not cry, do not cry, now is no time for tears.

Within her poor chest, against which she cradles

the shawl containing her beloved little cargo, within her panting, heaving breast, the woodcutter's wife feels her heart pound and pound and pound, then suddenly skip a beat. A sharp pain cuts her legs from under her, takes her breath away. She knows, she senses, that the hunters of the heartless are already tracking her, to snatch away her cherished little cargo.

She longs to stop, to fall to earth, to melt, to merge with the ferns, dissolve into the high grasses as, tighter and tighter, she hugs the little one she so loves. But fox cubs stand guard at her feet. They run, they run, they run, they are inured to running, to pursuing and to being pursued. They run, they tear up the ground, they run without fear, without reproach. Where? Where are they running to? Have no fear, they know how to get there, they know the path, the path to salvation.

Then, suddenly, the poor woodcutter's wife and her precious little cargo find themselves on the edge of a part of the wood so dense it is considered impenetrable by all. The fox cubs, for their part, do not slacken their pace, they plunge into the thicket, bounding from root to root, knocking against the low branches, tripping over the dead branches that litter the ground.

Then a voice, a voice at once feared and hoped for, rings out:

'Who goes there?'

'The poor woodcutter's wife,' she cries, as the fox cubs scamper on.

'What does she want, the poor woodcutter's wife?'

'Sanctuary! Sanctuary for me and for my . . . gift from the gods.'

The voice comes again:

'I heard gunshots, were they aimed at you?'

'They wanted . . . they wanted to . . . they wanted to take . . .'

'Step forward! Walk without fear!'

'They wanted to . . .' The poor woodcutter's wife is out of breath. Her voice deserts her, her legs give way. Even the fox cubs come to a halt, thwarted by the roots, by the brambles, by exhaustion.

The poor woodcutter's wife longs to tell all to the man with the rifle and the goat and the broken face, to tell of her fears, of the heartless, and of the axe. She tries again, with difficulty:

'They wanted to . . . They wanted to take . . . so my poor woodcutter husband . . . and his axe . . . and he . . .'

The man appears.

'You need say no more, I know the blackness of men's hearts, your husband and his axe did their valiant best. And if your tormentors warrant it, I too will do my valiant best.'

He shifts his rifle from one shoulder to the other and reaches out his arms.

'Give me your precious cargo and follow.'

The poor woodcutter's wife tenders the child, and the old man with his rifle with his goat and his shattered face receives her with a gentle dignity befitting one carrying a sacred object.

All three advance in silence. A clearing opens in the dense forest to reveal a garden that the poor woodcutter's wife has never seen. She received her daily ration of milk on the outskirts of the forest, and it was there, too, that she deposited her bundle of sticks.

In this late spring, in this early summer, the fruit on the trees seems to stretch out towards the child. The flowers stand tall, offering themselves up to be picked, as though to comfort the poor woodcutter's wife and her daughter. The gods are just on this side of the forest she thinks, yes, the gods can do good when they reflect and choose to do so.

Still cradling the child, the man walks towards a cabin, a cabin fashioned from logs just like her own, which stands next to a rock. He does not go into the cabin, but heads straight for the rock and steals into a grotto in which a diminutive goat with large swollen udders gambols about in joy at this visit.

The man with the rifle and the shattered face then sets the child down facing the goat. They are the same height. The man introduces them in this fashion: 'Daughter of the gods, this is your wet-nurse, your third mother.'

The delighted child hugs the goat which melts

into her arms, gazing into that distance where goats are wont to gaze. Then they bring their heads together and stand motionless, goat and girl, staring into each other's eyes, forehead pressed to forehead, as the poor woodcutter's wife sobs and the man with his gun and his goat and his shattered face whispers: 'Why do you cry, poor woodcutter's wife, now you shall have all the milk you need for her, and you will no longer have to gather kindling. Granted, I lose a bundle of firewood, but I gain a playmate for my lonesome goat, so all four of us are better off. In this mortal world, to gain something is to lose a little something in the process, be it the life of a loved one, or one's own.'

17

Day followed day, train followed train. In the overcrowded wagons, humanity lay dying. And humanity pretended to ignore it. Trains came and went from every vanquished city in that ravaged continent, but the poor woodcutter's wife was no longer there to see them.

They came and went, night and day, day and night, and no one showed the slightest interest. No one heard the cries of the transported, the sobs of mothers mingling with the death-rattles of the old men, the prayers of the credulous, the whimpers and the terrified screams of children separated from parents who had already surrendered to the gas.

18

And then, and then, the trains ceased to run. And having ceased to run, they ceased to deliver their wretched cargo of shaven heads. No more trains, no more shaven heads. Meanwhile, our hero, former father of twins, former husband to his beloved wife, now suddenly a former shaver of heads, collapsed, overcome by starvation, sickness and despair. Around him, the scant survivors who were still conscious murmured: 'We must hold on, hold on, hold on, and hold on some more, it is sure to end in the end, already we can hear the distant roar of cannons.' A comrade even whispered into the canal of his ear, 'The Reds are coming, the Death's Heads will end up shitting in their boots.'

In the meantime, those same Death's Heads forced them to dig trenches in the snow so they could burn the glut of corpses piled high around the crematoria which they were forced to hastily destroy so that, along with these surviving witnesses, they might eliminate every trace of their monstrous crime. Hair that only yesterday had been so prized went unharvested. Worse still, the hair that was already packed, ready for use, went unshipped. It piled up, abandoned, next to the mountains of spectacles, wedged between the heaps of men's, women's, and children's clothes. They too had to disappear.

Hold on, hold on, hold on, it is sure to end in the end. Now, he too longed to disappear, to end, to end, to end. Night and day, he was delirious. As he tramped though the snow, he was delirious, as he dug, he was delirious, remembering, worse still, reliving the fatal moment when he had torn one of his twins from his wife's arms, endlessly reliving that moment when he had tossed the child from the train into the snow. That snow through which he now plodded, plodded as he dug the hole where he in turn would eventually be burned. Why, why, why that frantic, fatal gesture? Why not accompany his wife and their two children to the end, to the ends of this journey? To rise together, the four of them together, to rise into the heavens in plumes of smoke, dark, oily smoke. Suddenly, he collapsed. At the risk of their own lives, two comrades dragged him into a nearby shack so that he would not be hurled, still half-alive, into the flames.

When he regained consciousness, he felt at ease here in this shack, amid the piled corpses. He found it an appropriate place to wait for death, for deliverance, at the end.

19

Death did not come and deliverance appeared in the guise of a young soldier wearing a red star whose bulging eyes bore witness to the horrors he had just discovered. Having realized that the corpse staring at him was still alive, the young starred soldier pressed the mouth of his canteen to those lips and biscuits into those hands, then gathered him in his arms, snatching him from the mass of death and laying him outside the shack on a patch of ground without corpses, beneath the reawakening spring sun.

In the very place that, only yesterday, was ruled by snow and boots and riding crops, by caps emblazoned with Death's Heads, the grass now grew, lush and thick, speckled with crowds of small white blossoms. It was then that he heard a bird sing, a hymn welcoming him back to life. And it was then that tears flowed from the eyes that had grown as dry, he thought, as his heart. The tears reminded him that he was a living being once more.

How did he find the strength to stand, to walk, and walk, and carry on walking? Had the song of the nightingale been enough to kindle the thought that his daughter, his beloved, unknown little daughter might also have survived? And that if she had survived, then he had a duty, a responsibility to do everything in his power, everything in his power to find her.

And so, he set off walking, following the Reds as they marched steadily west. He collapsed from starvation outside a church. He was helped to his feet by a priest who fed him, prayed for him. Then he set off again, walking, walking.

At length, he came to what was called a reunification camp filled with refugees and displaced people who had fled the Reds, only to be overtaken by their rapid advance. His ghostly appearance together with his number tattooed on his forearm served as his passport. Here, he had room and board, but no sooner had he settled in than he found himself reliving that fatal moment, the train, the snow, the forest, the prayer shawl, the old woman, and also the hope. But mostly, mostly, the eyes of his wife as she turned away from him forever and for always. Why, why had he not allowed fate to obliterate the four of them together, together?

The poor woodcutter's wife did not notice that the cargo trains no longer crisscrossed her forest, so enraptured was she by the sight of her little cargo, growing and thriving before her very eyes. The little girl was constantly laughing, singing, babbling and dancing with the goat that had become more than a sister to her, beneath the watchful gaze of the man with the rifle and the shattered face.

The poor woodcutter's wife could not remember ever experiencing such happiness in all the long, long course of her life. As for the man with the rifle, he kept a watchful eye, and kept his ear cocked to the east. He knew the Reds were advancing. He rejoiced even though he feared them. He feared the Reds as he had feared the grey-green of the Death's Heads with their minions and their collaborators. Once a week, he visited one of the villages that bordered the forest in order to barter his goat's cheese for basic necessities. There, people talked only of the looming end of this terrible war, with hope or with regret. Before long, planes emblazoned with red stars were bombing the positions of the Grey-Green, then the roar of cannonfire took over. The hunters of the heartless had gone to ground or had fled to the West.

Rifle in hand, the man with the shattered face patrolled the eastern flank of his fiefdom, determined that his right of property be respected by the new invaders. Two Red soldiers stole stealthily into the forest. Seeing a man armed with a rifle, they laid him low with a burst of machine-gun fire. Then, warily, one of the soldiers approached, turned the body over with the toe of his boot and, seeing nothing appealing in the man's face, shot his comrade-in-arms a disgusted look and said in a contemptuous voice: 'An old man, ugly.' Noting that the man lying on the ground was alone, they departed to re-join the main phalanx of Red Stars who had elected to skirt around the forest rather than go through it.

The following morning, after an anxious night, the poor woodcutter's wife discovered the body of the man with the shattered face and the tender heart. She wept bitterly, which caused her little cargo to weep too. Even the tender-eyed goat wept. Deciding not to bury it, the poor woodcutter's wife covered the body with blossoming branches then she contrived a prayer that expressed both her gratitude and her wish: may this good man finally find the peace and happiness denied him here on earth among the gods that welcome him. She thought about the gods of the train but did not mention them: she no longer trusted them.

She realized that if the child, her child, had

survived, it was no thanks to them, it was thanks to the hand that had dropped her from the train into the snow, it was thanks to the righteousness of the man with the rifle and the goat. 'May they be blessed,' she said at length.

She bundled up a few old clothes, carefully wrapped the freshly made cheese and the tools for making it in the prayer shawl and, taking her daughter by the hand, and leading the goat like a pack animal, set off. Not knowing where to go, she walked straight ahead, towards the East, the place where, they say, the sun still rises.

Along the way, she passed hundreds of tanks and trucks emblazoned with red stars. She wandered through countless ruined villages, and, after a time, she stopped on one of the village squares, chose a ruin that looked inviting, and there she settled. She spread the prayer shawl on a section of wall that was still standing, and on it laid the few cheeses that had survived and sat to wait for customers, her daughter comfortably settled on her lap while the little goat grazed on a bank.

20

In the so-called reunification camp former victims commingled and clashed with their former tormentors. The former seeking to 'start afresh' as people did not say in those days, the latter seeking to melt into the throng of refugees. Do not stay here, go, flee again, but go where? Where could he go, wondered our hero, former shaver of heads, former medical student, former father, former living creature turned shadow. Back to the country whence he came by train after being rounded up by the police of that same country? Which way to go? The North, the East, the West? And once there, take up his medical studies again?

Open a hairdressing salon so that he might impose upon the world a cropped, a close-cropped style, a fashion for shaven heads? No, no, besides he could not leave the region without knowing whether his daughter, his fragile little girl, his little ... what was her name again? What name had he given her? What was she called? He no longer knew, no longer remembered his daughter's name.

That same day, he left the camp, his pocket jingling with a pittance given by the camp authorities so that those wishing to leave could leave and thereby free up space by vacating the straw mattress they occupied. He walked, he walked, he walked some more, reaching for the railway, the forest, the bend in the line, the old woman kneeling in the snow. Finally, he found an abandoned railway line, already overgrown with weeds.

He followed these tracks. He came to a forest and carried on, he came to another, he carried on, he came to another. There was no longer any snow, nothing seemed familiar except the old women who never responded to his greeting. It was like looking for a needle in a haystack. He abandoned the railway which had already been abandoned by its trains and wandered through towns and villages. Everywhere celebrations were in full swing. The war was over for everyone, except for him and his kin.

There were songs, and flags, and speeches, even fireworks, all this folly, all this joy reminded him that he was alone, he would for ever be alone, alone in mourning the dead, alone in grieving for humanity, in grieving for the slaughtered, in grieving for his wife, his children, his parents, her parents. He passed through towns and villages like an apparition, a witness to celebration, to jubilation, to salutes, to oaths: never again, never again.

He did not know precisely what he was looking for. He simply walked. He felt his head spin and remembered that he was hungry. In spite of everything, he was hungry. On a little table he saw cheeses, tiny cheeses, and suddenly he longed for some cheese. These little cheeses were laid out on a curious tablecloth ill-suited to displaying cheese, a cloth that seemed to be embroidered with threads of gold and silver. He laid a hand on the cloth, set down a few coins and suddenly, suddenly, he realized. Then he looked up at the old woman, who was not so old, seated behind the little table covered with this curious cloth. The woman had a child in her lap. They both smiled at him and seemed to be encouraging him to pick one of the cheeses. The old woman spoke to him in a language he did not understand. She gestured for him to help himself, but he had eyes only for the little girl. The child, too, gestured with her eyes, her hands, for him to help himself, she praised the quality, then pointed to the goat next to her, indicating that the cheeses were born from the milk of this goat. He did not understand everything, but he understood the gist. His daughter, this was his daughter, the daughter thrown from the train, the daughter destined for the ovens, the daughter that he had saved.

A cry, a terrible cry, a cry of joy, of grief, of triumph, a cry took shape within his chest but no sound, no sound came from his lips. He snatched up a cheese, still staring at the little girl, his little girl. She was alive, she was alive, she was happy, she was smiling. He too gave the ghost of a smile, then reached out a trembling hand towards the little girl's cheek, to stroke this tempting cheek. The girl grabbed his hand and pressed it to her lips before bursting into laughter. He quickly pulled his hand away.

Feeling uneasy, he stepped back, still gazing at the old woman, the goat, and the little girl he had just brought into the world a second time. With searing intensity, he gazed at this cheesemonger and his own girl sitting on her lap, kissing her. He stared intently as though to burn onto his pupils, his heart, his soul this image of their shared happiness. Why reveal himself? Why upset the balance? What did he have to offer his own daughter? Nothing, less than nothing. He took a few steps more then stopped again. Perhaps, after all, he should . . . perhaps he might . . . then with a superhuman effort of mingled joy and sorrow, he tore himself away. He strode off quickly.

He had vanquished death, he had saved his daughter with a senseless act, he had triumphed over the monstrous extermination machine. He summoned the courage to take one last look at the daughter he had found and lost again for ever. Already, she was singing the praises of the cheeses to a new customer, her tiny gesticulating hands explaining its provenance, pointing from the little goat to her beloved mother.

Come, it is time that we left our little cargo and allowed her to live her life. Sorry? You want to know what happened to her former father? People say – but people say so many things – that he went back to the country where he and his wife and his two young children were rounded up together with thousands of other men, women and children, people say that he went back there and completed his medical studies, that he became a paediatrician, that he devoted his life to looking after and caring for the children of others.

The little cargo, for her part, grew up to be a

young pioneer. She was given a red scarf and also a red star that she could pin to her white blouse. A photo of her appeared on the cover of a magazine, she looked radiant. The photographer had asked her to smile.

People even say – though, as I've said, people say so many things – that the great doctor, while visiting that country – for every year he came to commemorate the anniversary of the liberation of the camp that had swallowed up his wife and one of his children, along with his parents and those of his wife – people say that he saw the photograph and he felt as though he recognized his wife and his own mother, people even say that that he wrote to the state magazine *Youth and Joy* to try to contact the young pioneer Maria Tchekolova, who had been presented as the most deserving pioneer, being the daughter of a poor woman, a poor woodcutter's wife who had become a cheesemonger.

No, we know nothing, or at least I personally have heard nothing about the success or failure of this attempt made by the former father of twins. We therefore do not know, and we will never know, whether or not he was finally reunited with his daughter.

Epilogue

There. Now you know everything. Sorry? Another question? You want to know if this is a true story? A true story? Of course not, absolutely not. There were no cargo trains crossing a war-torn continent to deliver urgently their oh-so-perishable cargo. No reunification camps, internment camps, concentration camps, or even extermination camps. No families vaporized in smoke after their final journey. No shorn hair, gathered, packaged and shipped. There were no flames, no ashes, no tears. None of this, none of this happened, none of this is true. Any more than the poor woodcutter and her poor woodcutter husband, any more than the heartless and the hunters of the heartless. None of this, none of this is true. Not the liberation of the towns and the fields, the forests and the camps, which never existed. Nor the years that followed that liberation. Not the grief of fathers and mothers searching for their missing children. Not even the fringed prayer shawls woven from gold and silver threads. Not the man with the goat and the shattered face, nor the man who wore – thanks be to God, if indeed He still exists! – nor the man who wore a mole that had been disembowelled and turned inside out to make a hat. None of this, none of this is true. Not the poor woodcutter's axe, the axe that sliced the mole in two before dispatching the two wretched militiamen, hunters of the heartless.

None of this, none of this is true.

The one thing that is true, genuinely true, or deserves to be in the context of this story, because there must be a grain of truth in any story otherwise why sweat blood to tell it, the one true thing, *truly* true, is that a little girl – who did not exist – was thrown from the window of a cargo train, out of love and out of despair, was thrown from a train, wrapped in a fringed prayer shawl embroidered with gold and silver thread –a prayer shawl that did not exist – was tossed into the snow at the feet of a poor woodcutter's wife with no children to treasure, and that this poor woodcutter's wife –who did not exist – gathered her up, fed her, treasured her and loved her more than anything. More than life itself. There.

Appendix for lovers of true stories

Convoy number 45 left Drancy on 11 November 1942 with seven hundred and seventy-eight men, women and children aboard, many of them elderly and infirm, among them a blind man, Naphtali Grumberg, the author's grandfather.

Two survivors in 1945.

Convoy 49 set off on 2 March 1943, carrying a thousand Jews including Zacharie Grumberg, the author's father, and Sylvia Menkès, born on 4 March 1942, and gassed on 4 March 1943, the anniversary of her birth.

In 1945, six survivors, including two women.

The Memorial to the Deportation of Jews from

France, set down in 1978 by Serge Klarsfeld from the alphabetical lists of Jews deported from France, serves for many of us, children of the *déportés*, as a family vault. According to the book, Abraham and Chaja Wiesenfeld, and their twin girls, Fernande and Jeannine, born in the tenth arrondissement of Paris on 9 November 1943, departed Drancy on 7 December of that same year, twenty-eight days after their birth. Convoy number 64 (see Klarsfeld *op. cit.*).

A Note from the Translator

The Most Precious of Cargoes is a fable so delicate yet so harrowing that when I began my translation, I was terrified I would break the spell. Translation is never simply a matter of words; it is about listening for voice, being attentive to cadence and to rhythm, to the silences between words. From the horrors of war, Jean-Claude Grumberg has woven a fable as beautiful and intricate as the prayer shawl at the heart of the story, fine threads of allegory and history, of love and devastating loss. In translating it, I have endeavoured to preserve its simplicity and its jarring beauty, braiding the leitmotifs of fairy tale and fable as they play out in the omnipresent shadow of the Shoah. Theodor Adorno famously said, 'There can be no poetry after Auschwitz,' but out of his own grief Jean-Claude Grumberg has fashioned something lyrical and beautiful from the ashes.

—Frank Wynne